FROM ROTARY
IN HONOR OF OUR SPEAKER

Derek Hutchy

11/9/2017
DATE

For my parents

ISBN 978-0-06-222916-8 (trade bdg.)

The artist used fabric, watercolor, pen and ink, and a variety of media to create flat images and three-dimensional scenes,
which were photographed and digitized to create the illustrations for this book.
Design and typography by Martha Rago. Hand lettering by Stephen Rapp.
15 16 17 18 19 SCP 10 9 8 7 6 5 4 3 2 1

First Edition

HAPPY HALLOWEEN, WITCH'S CAT!

Harriet Muncaster

HARPER
An Imprint of HarperCollinsPublishers

My mom is a witch,
and I am her special witch's cat.
She is a good witch,
and together we are just right.

COSTUME St

Halloween is coming!

What will I be?

A green frog?

Too slimy!

Maybe a silver skeleton?

Too bony!

How about a pink ballerina?

Too frilly!

Or a **black** vampire?

Too toothy!

A yellow mummy?

Too tangly!

An orange pumpkin?

Too smiley!

I know! A white ghost!

Too spooky!

Nothing feels right, so we go home for supper.

Just before bed,
I have the best idea of all.

"Mom," I say, "I will be a witch, and you can be my special witch's cat!"